# BROCK

## ALL THE SINGLE DADS BOOK FOUR

SADIE KING

# ALL THE SINGLE DADS

These single dad hotties are fiercely protective and will do anything for the ones they love.

The series features grumpy single dads, secret billionaires, shy neighbors, and men turned obsessive by the curvy heroines who capture their hearts.

Each book in the series is a standalone but best enjoyed together. And look out for your favorite characters from Maple Springs popping in for cameo appearances.

**All the Single Dads**

*Jaxon* – Kali & Jaxon

*Jake* – Fiona & Jake

*Levi* – Aria & Levi

*Brock* – Olive & Brock

*Anton* – Eden & Anton

*Xavier* – Angela & Xavier

BROCK

ALL THE SINGLE DADS BOOK FOUR


**Brock**


When you're left with baby twins to raise on your own, there's not a lot of time for romance. At least that's what I've told myself for the last four years.

However, their sweet and perky daycare worker has been getting into my dreams and making me think it's time to end my lonely spell.

But when she rejects me, I will stop at nothing to make her mine.


**Olive**


I'm going for the daycare director position. So, I definitely should not get involved with the hot single dad who's been pursuing me relentlessly.

Unless we do it secretly.

That's the thing about doing something you shouldn't, it always feels so darn good.

But if anyone found out… My career would be over.


*Brock* is a forbidden love romance featuring a single dad and curvy woman who's off limits.

www.authorsadieking.com

# BROCK

As soon as we pull into the parking lot my eyes flick over the figures milling about the day-care center. It's all parents, tugging on the hands of children and babies clutched to chests.

I can't see Olive and my breath hitches in my throat. I get out of the car and scan the steps.

The door is propped open and a figure crouches in the opening, half turned toward the entrance, one eye level with a small boy.

He can't be over two years old. He's crying, unwilling to let go of his mother's hand. The crouching woman opens her arms and scoops him up as she stands. She spins around with the boy, a wide smile on her face, her blonde hair catching in the morning sun.

It's her... Olive. I feel my body relax and I can breathe again.

Her eyes sparkle at the little boy and it's infectious.

He giggles and reaches a chubby hand for her silky hair.

"I don't blame you buddy," I mutter under my breath.

"What did you say daddy?"

I glance into the car at Sophie, looking up at me expectantly from her car seat.

"Nothing sweetie."

I open the back door distractedly, still looking at Olive.

With the boy firmly in hand they wave goodbye to the mom and head inside. The boy seems happy now, Olive's smiling demeanor taking the sting out of parting with his mom.

I watch her skirt swish round her hips as she disappears inside.

"I want to get out."

This time it's Sarah, kicking the back of the seat impatiently.

"All right girls, give me a minute."

I get Sophie out of her car seat first. Sarah stares at me sullenly when I come around to her side of the car.

"You always get Sophie down first. I want to go first."

I raise my eyebrows at her, not giving in to her pouts. "I think you were the first to get your ice-cream yesterday so that can't be true."

"Humph."

It's hard having twins. Especially raising them on

your own. But I'm used to their moods now and know it will pass.

I get the bags out the trunk and grasp their little hands in mine as we navigate the parking lot full of SUVs doing the morning drop off.

By the time we reach the stairs leading up to the daycare center, Sarah is smiling again and giggling with her sister.

Olive hasn't come back yet. It's her sour faced colleague, Lindy, who gives me a long slow once over as I approach with the girls.

She smooths her hair down and pushes her chest out.

"Good morning, Brock."

She lowers her lashes at me and swings her hips. She's so obvious it's almost comical.

It annoys me she's flirting with me in front of my girls. I know that's hypocritical because I want to flirt with her colleague, Olive. But anger flares inside me all the same.

"Morning," I say curtly.

She looks down at the girls and they squirm under her gaze. "Morning girls, did you have a good weekend with your daddy?"

Sophie nods happily but Sarah just stares at her. I smile inwardly at my moody girl who can be difficult sometimes but she isn't fooled by anyone.

I check my watch as if I have somewhere to be, but really, I don't want to talk to Lindy. I'm annoyed that I missed Olive, and I hope she might come out again after settling the little boy in.

"I want to show you my drawing."

Sophie takes Lindy's hand and I could kiss my daughter and her perfect timing. She drags Lindy down the hall and Sarah follows. Sarah turns to wave goodbye and make a face behind Lindy's back. I should tell her off but it makes me laugh and fills me with such parental pride. My two girls, sunshine and darkness and both wonderful in their own way.

I know it's not cool to hang around at a preschool, but I take my phone out and pretend to check my messages, hoping Olive will come back.

And in a few moments, I'm rewarded. I hear the swish of her long skirt and look up to find her standing in the doorway her arms folded and her eyebrows raised.

"You going to stand here and wait for them all day?"

She's smiling and I know she's thinking of the first week I dropped the girls off. I was so nervous about leaving the babies, of not having them with me, that I waited in the car all morning. I did that for the following three days until Olive came out and knocked on the car window startling me out of sleep.

I chuckle and slip my phone in my pocket. "I know they're in good hands."

She's watching me with her sparkling eyes and smiling mouth and I've never seen her look so beautiful.

At first, I didn't notice the sweet teacher who looked after my girls every day. I was exhausted and still grieving.

Eventually the grief subsided, the girls grew into toddlers and I started getting more sleep. I looked forward to the daycare drop offs and pickups just so I could talk to the smiling teacher with the soft curves and dancing eyes.

I've been watching her from afar, and I notice her eyes light up when she sees me. It's subtle, not like her colleague, who tries to put on a sexy demeanor.

I realized a few months ago how my feelings for Olive had grown, and I'm sure she feels it to.

I've not dated since my wife died while giving birth to the twins. The grief was too overwhelming, but slowly, my wife's memory grew more distant. Now it's Olive's face I see when I lie in bed. Olive's voice I hear in my dreams, and on the long nights in bed alone, it's Olive I think of.

My heart races as I open my mouth to speak. I've gotten out of practice with women and the words don't come easy.

"Olive…" Her smile fades at my serious tone.

I take a step closer to her and she glances around nervously. There's no one else in the parking lot now. The kids have been delivered and the parents have left.

"I want to take you out."

A pink flush creeps up her neck and she lowers her

eyes. It's an agonizing moment as I wait for her to speak.

Slowly she raises her eyes to meet mine, but instead of the happiness I expect to see, they're full of turmoil, not sparkling like I'd hoped.

"Let me take you out to dinner sometime."

She shakes her head slowly and takes a step back.

"I can't. I'm sorry."

It's not the response I was expecting. I've felt this pull toward her and I'm sure she's felt it too. Her rejection is like a blow to the chest.

There's the sound of children singing from inside and she glances toward the door. "I've got to go."

I nod and she turns, her skirt swishing around her ankles. The door shuts behind her and I'm left out in the cold wondering how the hell I read the situation so wrong.

# OLIVE

My stomach churns as I walk away from Brock. The moment I've been simultaneously hoping for and dreading has just happened; he asked me out.

Inside my heart is doing a happy dance, knowing that I haven't been imagining the growing attraction between us, that my instincts were right.

But that's no consolation for the fact I had to turn him down. That dating him would put my whole future at risk.

It makes me feel sick knowing I had to turn down the man I've been pining for ever since he turned up exhausted and anxious with two babies.

Lindy's leaning against the office door, eyeing me suspiciously.

"What did pretty boy want?"

She doesn't hide the fact that she lusts after Brock. I

slide past her into the office and go to the supplies cupboard, hoping she doesn't see the flush I can feel creeping up my neck.

"He asked about the girls going to the toilet on their own." It's a lie and Lindy squints at me suspiciously.

"They've been toilet trained for over a year."

I shrug. "Had a relapse apparently. It happens."

I grab a bunch of paints and brushes and look around for the aprons.

I'm not sure why she's hanging about in the office and not in class where she should be, but I know better than to question Lindy. She's the owner's daughter and thinks it means she can do as she pleases.

"I wonder if he's got a big dick?"

"Lindy!" I glance around to make sure kids aren't within hearing distance. "You can't talk like that in a nursery."

She rolls her eyes are me. "Relax. The kids wouldn't know what I was talking about."

But there's something else that's angered me. The way she's talking about Brock like he's some piece of meat.

"And it's disrespectful."

She snorts. "Come on, lighten up."

Brock has had a hard time bringing up twins on his own. From what I've seen of him over the last four years, he's a kind father, tired, and harried and doing his best. He's sensitive and loving to his girls and they adore him.

To have someone like Lindy objectify him makes my skin crawl.

"No, I won't lighten up. He's one of our parents and should be respected."

She raises her eyebrows at me.

"Oh Olive, don't tell me you like him?"

She's behaving like we're at high school and not senior nursery workers at a respected day care center.

I shake my head quickly but I can't look her in the eye.

I see the aprons bunched in a corner, no doubt left there by Lindy and not hung up properly.

"Don't be ridicules, he's a parent. We should show them respect, that's all."

I grab the aprons and go to push past her but she steps in front of me a triumphant look in her eyes.

"You do fancy him. What would the board say?"

I keep my expression neutral, trying with every fiber of my being not to betray the turmoil that's going on inside. Because she's hit it in one.

The position of daycare director has come down to the two of us.

I've been working toward this my whole working life. I've taken a management course, planed the activities for the kids, and been a mentor for the junior day care workers. It should be a clear-cut decision. Except that the board will look for any excuse to cut me out and give the owner's daughter the position.

Which is why I turned down Brock. I must be

squeaky clean, or Lindy will end up running this place. For the sake of the kids, I can't have that.

"They can say what they like because it's not true. I talk to Brock like I talk to any of the parents. We have a professional relationship and nothing more."

I stand up straight as I say it and look her directly in the eye, because every word is true. My heart may yearn for him, but I know what getting involved with someone, especially someone who's considered one of our vulnerable parents, would look like. It would be career suicide.

Lindy looks me up and down and makes a harrumph sound.

"All right, Miss integrity," she says it mockingly like it's a bad thing. "I'm still gonna get this job though. Daddy will make sure of it."

She tosses her hair and flounces off. I watch her go, wondering if she's delusional or if I am. Giving her this job would be the worst thing for the center and the kids. I hope the board sees that.

3

# BROCK

$\mathcal{I}$'m still thinking about Olive two nights later as I sip a beer at The Blue Boar.

I'm not sure why she rejected me when we so clearly have a connection. Unless I'm imagining it. It's been a long time since I felt something for a woman, maybe I'm out of touch.

Then I think about her warm smile and those sparkling eyes that light up when she sees me. Nah, I'm not imagining that.

"What do you think Brock?"

I'm jolted back into the present by Jake, looking at me expectantly.

"Sorry man, what was that?"

"Hockey or soccer? What are you gonna get your girls into?"

I shrug. "Whatever they want, as long as it's not cheerleading."

"Amen to that."

He holds his beer bottle up and I tap the neck with mine.

"There's no way I'm gonna let Riley be ogled by every horny high school boy in town."

I nod my agreement.

My neighbor is babysitting the girls so I can come out and meet my buddies. It was Olive who first mentioned the Single Dad Group to me, hesitantly, that first week of nursery when she found me sleeping in my car. The girls were already six months old and I wish I'd found these guys sooner.

They were my lifeline when the twins were babies. Giving out advice on feeding and nap time and making sure I was getting enough sleep.

These days the meet ups are more out of habit. We've become good friends and as the kids have gotten older, we've each found our own way.

Now it's our turn to give out advice. The group organizer, Xavier has just adopted a little boy and he looks as sleep deprived as I remember. I've offered to stop round on the weekend to give him a bit of a break. The girls love babies and we can look after the little guy while he gets some time to himself.

Tonight, there's a game on the big screen which is why the conversation has turned to kids' sports.

Anton tells us about his boy's latest basketball wins but I can't stay focused. My mind goes back to Olive, wondering what I'm missing.

I'm facing the door and as I bring my beer to my lips, I see a movement that makes me pause. The swish of a long skirt and blonde hair.

I leave my beer on the table and hurry to the door.

Jake calls after me but I ignore him as I rush out into the night.

It's Olive, walking away from me down the street. I'd recognize the sway of those hips anywhere.

"Olive," I call, but she doesn't hear me.

I jog after her and she turns down an alleyway that leads to the carpark behind the bar.

"Olive."

This time she turns and her hands fly to her chest.

"Brock, you startled me."

I catch up to her in the alleyway. "What are you doing walking down here on your own?"

It comes out harsher than I meant it to but it's dark down the alleyway with no streetlights. Anything could happen.

Her eyes sparkle. "Are you concerned for my safety? That's sweet." She holds a set of keys up. "I parked through there."

Her lips are curled up in a smile and her eyes are dancing. She looks beautiful and expectant. Probably wondering where the hell I came from.

"I was just in the Blue Boar and I saw you walk past." I say as way of explanation. "How about you?"

"I just had dinner with a friend."

The words cut to my heart and I'm instantly jealous.

"A boyfriend?" It comes out more aggressively than I meant. But it just makes her more amused.

"No, an old friend from school." She tilts her head and studies me. "Are you jealous?" She says it teasingly but my hairs are standing on end.

"Damn right I'm jealous."

I take a step closer to her. My heart is thumping in my chest and the blood is running hot in my veins.

"I like you, Olive, I like you a lot."

She tilts her chin back and looks at me. I can see the rise and fall of her chest as her breathing gets ragged.

I sweep a strand of hair off her face and her skin is so smooth I must touch it again. I take her chin in my hand as I move closer to her, backing her up against the wall.

"Brock, we can't."

It comes out breathlessly. Her pupils dilate and her lips part. Her body wanting something different than her words.

I lean into her, taking in the sweet scent of her and I brush my lips against her neck.

"I want you, Olive."

I feel her breath hitch and her pulse races under my lips.

She whimpers, a short sharp sound that makes my balls pull up tight and all the blood rush to my dick.

"Can I kiss you?"

I bring my gaze round to hers, needing to see her

response, her consent. She's breathing heavily and her eyes are half closed.

She nods and I sweep my lips against hers. It's gentle, but her lips push forward to meet mine. Her eyes flutter open and I see the need in them, the desire.

I kiss her properly, and she responds, her tongue pushing into my mouth.

Her hands go around my neck and tangle in my hair. I press my body against hers, grinding her into the alleyway.

She responds like I knew she would. Her body craving this as much as mine. I trail my lips down her neck.

"Olive," I murmur, "We need to be together."

She stiffens and I pull away immediately, cursing myself for saying the wrong thing.

"What is it?"

Her eyes are hooded in the darkness, but she looks serious.

"I can't be with you Brock. I can't do this."

She puts her hands on my chest, and I step away giving her space.

"Why not? It's obvious it's what we both want."

She shakes her head. "It's not that simple." She hugs herself with her arms and I wait for her to continue.

"I can't get involved with a parent from the center, it would be unprofessional."

I take in what she's saying. Her job could be at risk.

But it's a whole year until the girls go to school. I'm not willing to wait that long.

"I'll move the girls, find them another preschool."

She shakes her head sadly. "You know how much they love it there. They've got friends. You wouldn't do that to them."

I know she's right. They love the teachers and the other kids.

"Is it really that bad to have a relationship, I mean, it's a proper relationship I want with you Olive, this isn't a casual thing."

Her breath hitches and she lowers her head.

"I'm in the running for the daycare director position. I'm up against Lindy, I can't have anything that will give the board an excuse not to hire me."

She looks up at me with sad eyes. And I see the conflict in them. She's got integrity, and I admire that.

I nod slowly.

"Thanks for understanding, Brock. I knew you would."

She gives my hand a quick squeeze before she turns and walks down the alley. I watch her until she's safely in her car.

If she thinks I'm letting her go that easily then she doesn't know me at all.

4

# OLIVE

The next day is Friday and I'm walking home from work with a heavy heart. I stayed late at work coming up with a new activity plan. Which meant I could hide in the office and avoid the parents collecting their kids. Well, avoid one parent in particular: Brock.

It felt so right kissing him last night and so wrong turning him away. My body hasn't forgiven me and I spent a restless night tossing and turning, thinking about his lips on mine. How good it would feel to give in to him.

I cross the road to my street and a shiver runs down my spine, as if someone's watching me. I turn quickly but there's no one there, only traffic moving slowly past the intersection.

I keep walking and there it is again, the feeling of being watched.

I walk faster. I can see my house in the next block and I get my keys out, ready. I clutch them between my fists, like I was taught in self-defense class, with the sharp bit poking out.

A car pulls up alongside me. With my heart in my throat, I glance to the driver's seat.

I'm flooded with relief as I see Brock.

"You scared me."

"Sorry, I needed to be well away from the center."

He nods at the passenger seat. "Get in."

My pulse flutters. I know I should keep walking but he's hard to resist.

"I can't be seen with you, Brock."

He grins. "Then we won't be seen."

I look up and down the street. It's almost empty, aside from an elderly lady walking her dog. No one from the center would see me here.

Without thinking about it too much, I scoot round to the passenger side and get in.

He pulls away from the curb.

It's thrilling to be in the car with him, like I'm doing something I shouldn't, and I never do anything I shouldn't.

"Where are you taking me?"

"To dinner. Like I wanted to."

Dinner is dangerous, anyone could see us in town. I open my mouth to protest but he's anticipated my concerns.

"Relax, dinner is at my house."

I breathe a sigh of relief. We won't be seen that way. "Where are the girls?"

"They're at their grans for the weekend."

"You've got it all figured out, haven't you?"

He grins. "I want you Olive, even if it means working hard to get you."

His words send a warmth spreading through me. He's not giving up on me easily, so maybe I should give in to him.

My body tingles at the thought and I feel a spasm of heat between my legs. It's not just dinner with him I'm looking forward to, it's what happens after.

His hand rests lightly on my thigh and the heat between my legs intensifies.

"You didn't think I'd let you go that easily, did you?"

I sit back in the seat and enjoy the drive. My body is tingling in anticipation and there's something else. The feeling that I'm doing something I shouldn't, that I'm breaking the rules, and for once in my life, I don't care.

Throughout dinner I've not been able to get my hands off Olive. Now that I've got her in my house, I need to touch her, to possess her.

My hand caresses her thigh as she finishes dessert. She's telling me about her family, and I am listening but I keep getting distracted by the way her mouth closes around the spoon. As I watch, she drags the spoon through her lips, pulling off the remaining ice cream and chocolate sauce.

Damn, she's sexy and she's not even aware of it.

The blood pulses through my veins and I push my chair back, unable to stand the pressure anymore.

She looks startled as I take her hands in mine.

"Dinner is finished."

I pull her up from her chair and she meets my gaze. There's uncertainty there, mixed with desire.

I bring her hands to my lips and kiss her fingers.

"Brock, we shouldn't…"

My kiss moves up her arm to her elbow and then to the nape of her neck. She tilts her head so I can brush her throat with my lips.

"We really shouldn't do this." It's more of a moan then a protest.

"Uh huh?" I murmur into her neck. "I'll stop anytime you want me to, just say the words."

I feel her pulse quicken under my lips.

"That's the problem, I don't want you to stop."

"Then I won't. I won't stop until you're crying out my name."

She gasps and I slide my hand up her body, pulling at the buttons on her blouse, suddenly needing to touch her all over.

The blouse sides off and I run my hands over her breasts, the weight of them feels good in my hands and I pull her bra down so I can clasp her nipples. They turn hard under my fingers and her breathing comes out heavy and ragged.

"We really shouldn't be doing this," she murmurs, even as her hands run over the back of my neck, tangling in my hair, and pulling me toward her.

"You tell me to stop any time you want, Olive, and I'll stop."

In response she tilts her head back, giving me access to her throat.

I kiss her lips, her neck, the delicate skin of her throat, making my way down her chest. I run my tongue over her nipples. And she whimpers a sweet sound that makes my pulse race.

With one hand on the small of her back, I lead her over to the couch and push her gently backwards.

I lay her down on the couch and her skirt falls open, showing her thick thighs. My hand runs up her skirt until I find her warm panties, already damp.

I'm hungry for her now and I pull her panties down and toss them on the floor. Her thighs fall open and I kneel in the gap.

She's panting as I run my dick over her entrance, coating it in her glistening wetness. I line my cock up with her pussy, resting my tip in the folds of her.

"We shouldn't do this," she moans.

I sit back, pulling my dick away. "I'll stop if you want."

Her eyes fly open and her gaze is full of need. "No," she whines. "Brock, put it back."

I raise to my knees so she can see my cock, thick in my hand. I give it a stroke and her eyes go wide.

"Put what back?"

I'm teasing her, but I want her to say it. I want to hear filthy things coming out of her sweet mouth.

"Put your cock back."

The words make me shiver and a squirt of pre-cum dribbles onto my fingers.

"Put it back where?"

She's panting now, her hand grips my thigh.

"Put your cock in my pussy."

I shudder and almost lose it right there.

I slide back into place between her legs, finding her wet opening with my tip.

I let it rest there and she whines impatiently.

"You're missing a word."

She looks confused and slightly cross and so full of desire. It's making me crazy.

"Please," she groans. "Please Brock, put your cock in my pussy and fuck me."

As she says the last words, I slam into her. She buckles under me and I hold her hips. Her pussy squeezes me tight and she screams out my name.

I slide out and slam into her again, sending her body writhing.

"We really shouldn't do this." She pants as her hands grab my ass, pulling me deeper inside.

"You're right," I lean forward and whisper into her ear. "We shouldn't be fucking."

She moans as I say the words. "It's naughty, Olive, you're a bad girl."

Her eyes go wide and she lets out a high-pitched wail.

"You're a naughty girl, and I need to punish you."

I slide my dick right out of her and the looks she gives me is priceless.

"What are you doing?" She whines, disbelief, confusion crossing her face.

"You've been bad Olive, and I'm going to punish you."

She looks like she wants to hit me, so before she gets the chance, I flip her over so her stomach's pressed into the couch.

I flip her skirt up and she gasps as I expose her bare ass.

My hand comes down on her ass check and she squeals.

"You're bad Olive. You'd better give me that ass of yours, let me teach you a lesson."

She pushes her ass into the air and I pull her cheeks apart. Her pink pussy hole glistens as she pushes it toward me and I know I can't keep this up much longer.

I run my dick over her opening and she pushes back against me, wanting me to be inside her.

"Not so fast, Olive."

"Please Brock." She sways her ass and I can't resist that hole any longer.

"Please Brock, fuck me."

I push into her and she cries out as I sink in deep.

Her pussy squeezes my dick and I feel my balls pull up tight.

Her round ass is too tempting and I slap my hand against her cheek.

"You still think we shouldn't do this?" I hiss.

I'm pumping her hard now, needing to claim her.

"You're bad Olive, you've been a bad girl."

She's getting off on my words and it's the hottest thing I've ever seen.

My hand comes down on her ass again and she cries out, bucking into me at the same time.

"Brock!" She screams. Her pussy clenches around me and she's over the edge.

I slam into her once more and find the same release. It's powerful and sexy and I push into her until all my seed is spent.

Then I pull her close and kiss her gently.

She's mine now, whether it's right or wrong, she's all mine.

6

OLIVE

Two weeks later…

*H*is lips brush against mine and I feel the anxiety lesson a little.

"You'll be great today. They'll love you."

It's the day of the final interview for the daycare director position. I have to give a presentation to the board and then they'll ask questions.

"What if I forget what to say?"

He puts a warm steady hand on my fidgety one. "Just do it like we've been practicing and you'll be fine."

I take a deep breath.

"I hope so."

He gives my hand a reassuring squeeze. "Go get 'em tiger."

I grab my laptop bag from between my feet and push open the passenger door. Before I slide out,

Brock captures my chin and give me a slow calming kiss.

"You'll be great."

I'm so busy thinking about the presentation and making sure I've got everything I need that I don't notice the figure standing across the road, holding a mobile phone up.

We've been careful the last two weeks. Meeting secretly and only at each other's houses. Brock drops me off at my place in the mornings and even then, I always check the street before I get out of the car.

But today, he's dropped me at the hired rooms where the interview is taking place. He picked a side street, but I'm so preoccupied that I forget to check if anyone's watching.

It's not till I straighten up that I see her, Lindy.

She's standing at the end of the street with a full view of the driver's seat, a full view of Brock and the kiss we just shared.

She's got her arms folded and a smirk on her face as she strides toward the car.

"Well, well, Olive, I didn't think you were the type to get involved with our clients."

I take a step backward, dismay sweeping through me wondering how much she saw.

"I don't know what you mean."

She snorts. "I saw you kiss."

I shrug, trying to be causal. "Did you? Are you sure?"

If I put on an act maybe she'll doubt herself.

Her smirk turns to a chuckle. "Don't try to gaslight me, I have the evidence." She's been holding something in her hands and now lifts it in front of my face, her mobile phone.

"I'm sure the board will be interested to see this."

She hits play and on the screen is a quick zoom in as Brock leans forward to kiss me, a long slow kiss on the lips.

My heart sinks. She's got me.

"Having casual relations with one of the parents from the center? We can't have a director sleeping round with all the dads. That's not the morals we want to promote."

"I'm not sleeping around. It's not like that."

She looks amused. "Oh, you love him. How sweet."

My checks go red. Because yeah, she's right, I do love Brock.

I've loved him ever since he brought those two tiny babies into my care. That love has grown in the last two weeks. It's blossomed into something special, into something deep. I know instantly that I won't give him up.

"Yeah, I do love him, Lindy, and if that means I don't get the job then that's fine, at least I'll have Brock."

Her face screws up with bitterness and it hits me suddenly. This is about more than just the job. She's jealous.

"You think he loves you, then you're wrong." Her eyes narrow and I've never seen her look so nasty.

"You're not the only one he flirts with you know. Every time I see him, he flirts with me. He flirts with everyone. You're the only one stupid enough to sleep with him."

Anger flares up inside me because I know it's not true, is it? It couldn't be true. But I remember seeing her and Brock talking a lot, her head tilted back laughing.

At that moment Brock gets out of the driver's seat.

"That's enough Lindy." He says quietly.

I turn to look at him the question in my eyes. He's looking back at me intently and I know she's wrong. I know he's mine and only mine and that's all that matters.

"Go show the board Lindy. I don't care."

She turns with a flourish and flounces away. I sink back against the car and watch her go, knowing she's about to end my career.

# BROCK

The disappointment on Olive's face is breaking my heart. She slumps against the car looking defeated. She's worked so hard for this and I'll not let her throw it away.

"Don't let her get away with this."

She turns to me and the distraught look on her usually sparkling features breaks my heart.

"I don't see how I've got a chance now. The board will see that video of me kissing you, one of our parents in full daylight. They'll think I behaved inappropriately."

Her top lip wobbles and she swipes quickly at her eyes.

I hurry round to her side of the car and gently wipe a tear away with my thumb.

"Be careful. You'll ruin your makeup."

"It doesn't matter now. I may as well go home. Once

the board see that video, they won't want to see me."

I hate seeing her like this and I put an arm around her wanting to comfort her.

"Is it really so bad to have a relationship with me?"

"They'll think it's casual. Lindy will tell them it's casual, that you're a big flirt, that we're just playing around. It shouldn't matter but it will."

"But we're not playing around, this is serious, Olive, I love you."

It's the first time I've told her my feelings and her face lights up, for a moment forgetting her troubles.

"I love you too."

My heart swells at the words. Then her smile falters as she remembers her predicament.

"But try explaining that to the board."

My hand goes to my pocket and I slide out the little turquoise box I've been keeping safe there.

"I wanted to do this tonight, but I think it's better now."

I sink to one knee and her eyes go wide; her hands fly to her mouth.

"Olive, you're the sweetest, happiest, sexiest woman I know. Will you marry me?"

I pop open the lid of the box and hold up the ring.

"Brock, are you sure?"

"Of course, I'm sure, or I wouldn't ask."

"You can't just propose so I look good for the board."

"Oh honey, that's not the reason I'm proposing. I

bought this ring after that first night we spent together because I knew you'd be my wife. I was going to ask you tonight, but under the circumstances, it may as well be now."

Her eyes meet mine and there's love and hope emanating from them.

I'm still on my knees and a car goes past and beeps at us, shouting something indiscernible from the window.

"So, what do you say?"

"Yes! I say yes."

I slip the ring onto her finger and she throws her arms around me. Now there are happy tears running down her face.

I dab at them with my thumb.

"Now, you go in there and give them your best professional presentation. And if they bring up the video, which they will. You show them this ring and ask if it's a crime to kiss your fiancé in public."

"I hope not because I'm about to do it again."

Her lips press into mine and it's a long slow tender kiss. My hands slide down her back and I could go on but another car beeps at us.

"Go on, go get 'em."

She throws me a smile as she hurries off down the street. I watch her ass sway as she gains confidence with every stride.

That's my woman, and she's going in there to kick ass. I couldn't be prouder.

# EPILOGUE

## OLIVE

Five years later…

*B*rock's arms go around my body and he pulls me against him. I can feel his hardness through the sheets pressing against my back.

"Good morning," he murmurs into my hair.

He moves against me, rubbing his dick against me and causing a shiver to run between my thighs and tug at my core.

His hand slides between my legs and with one stoke I'm already damp.

With a great effort I scramble onto my elbows to see the bedside clock. "What time is it?"

He groans in response.

"We need to get the twins ready for school, and give the baby her bottle, and get our son dressed and fed. I need to get to the center early so I can unlock and set everything up."

"Relax." He pulls me down to the bed. "There's time."

His fingers push aside my panties and before I can protest any more, he slides a finger into me.

The sensation feels so good. I forget all the things we need to do and my mind goes blank.

"Why don't you climb up and take care of this hard on for me?"

"Brock, we really shouldn't…"

As I say the words, he slides my panties off and hitches my nightie up around my waist.

"I reckon we've got about five minutes 'til one of the kids burst in here, so you better work fast, sweetheart."

I straddle him, lining his cock up with my pussy and waste no time in sinking onto him. I slide down his shaft and feel him filling me up, empaling me.

He clings onto my ass as we rock back and forth. I lean forward, enjoying the pressure of his body against my clit.

My tits push against my nightie and he pulls the fabric down so he can capture my breast in his hands.

"That's it sweetheart, ride me hard and take what you need."

His words are too much for me and suddenly I'm over the edge. Muffling my cries against his neck.

He pulls me down on his cock, two hard, fast motions, then I feel him explode inside me.

We stay joined for a moment, rocking slowly before I roll off him.

We're still panting when the door opens and our three-year-old comes toddling into the room.

"I'm hungry." He climbs onto the bed and we make space for him between us.

The door opens again and it's the twins.

"Sophie's wearing the purple unicorn top I wanted to wear today," complains Sarah.

"I bagsed it last night. I'm wearing it."

Through the noise I hear cries from the room next door, signaling the baby is awake.

I slide out of bed with a look at my husband. He gives me a smile before he turns to the twins and enters negotiations about the unicorn top.

I go and fetch the baby; glad we shared a moment to ourselves before the chaos of family life.

WHAT TO READ NEXT

## THE BIKER'S REVENGE

**She's my enemy's daughter and my new obsession...**

After three years inside, there's only one thing I want: revenge.

But when a retaliation goes wrong, I find myself with a fire cat captive—Scarlett, my enemy's daughter.

She's half my age and dripping with innocence. Scarlett becomes my revenge, and it's never been sweeter. But when her father comes for her, there's no way I'm giving her up.

*The Biker's Revenge* is a forbidden love, age-gap romance that starts with a kidnapping and ends with a happily ever after. Featuring an OTT obsessed hero and the curvy girl he claims as his own.

Keep reading for an excerpt.

THE BIKER'S REVENGE

CHAPTER ONE

Bruno

The sound of smashing glass breaks the silence. Pans shakes out the rag that he wrapped around his wrist to break the window, sending shards of glass tumbling to the ground.

My eyes dart around the shadowy building, my ears straining for any sign that someone is inside.

But all is quiet at the Chaos Riders HQ. Our intel was correct. The club is on a run out of town, leaving their headquarters unprotected.

I don't expect to find much here, but we'll rough the place up, do as much damage as possible. I want Manny, the Chaos Riders' president, to know that I'm out, and I'm out for revenge.

I give a signal to the boys, and dark shapes emerge from the shadows. Pans is the first one in the window, and he clears the glass with a covered fist so no one gets cut as we climb through.

Flashing lights from the neon sign out front illuminate a bar with dancing poles leading up to the ceiling.

Lyle whistles. "Could get one of those installed at our place, Pres."

I shoot him a dark look. "You keep that in the strip club."

Lyle grins, but he knows I'm serious. My club is a place that's safe for women. There's a time and a place for a strip pole, and it's not front and center of our MC club.

"Where should we start?"

Jesse whistles softly as he twirls a baseball bat in his hand.

It's been a long time since I've been inside the Chaos Riders' clubrooms. It's been years since we were on friendly terms.

The floor's sticky, and empty beer bottles lay scattered on the floor. A thick layer of dust coats the framed pictures of bikes on the walls. The place stinks of vomit and stale beer, making my nose crinkle.

They don't take pride in their clubhouse the way we do. Maybe this little visit isn't going to hurt them too badly. But it's not about hurting them. It's about letting Manny know we're coming for him, letting him know that I'm out and I want my revenge.

"Anywhere you like. Smash it all to hell."

I swing my bat at the wall, feeling a surge of satisfaction as a portrait of Manny crashes to the ground.

The glass frame shatters, and I don't bother trying to muffle the sound.

The boys let out a whoop and let loose with their bats, swinging wildly at anything and everything.

I reckon we've got about five minutes before someone shows up, and I'm not going to waste that time.

Pulling my shoulder back, I swing as hard as I can, connecting with a pinball machine. It gives a strangled beep as the glass smashes. I hit it again and again, thinking about the last three years.

Three years in prison, locked up and away from my club and away from my daughter, Lily.

It's lucky I had the foresight to add Gina as one of her guardians. I did that ten years ago in case something ever happened to me so they couldn't take my daughter away.

My bat comes down on the legs of the pinball machine, and it gives a whine as a leg gives out and it sinks to its knees.

Smashing shit up feels good. I spin around, looking for my next target.

The room is in chaos with my guys joyfully destroying the clubhouse.

Lyle has rescued a bottle of bourbon from the bar, and he takes a swig before smashing the fridges in.

Someone's gone through to the kitchen, and there's the sound of pots and pans being thrown to the floor.

There's a staircase, and I head up there. I'm looking for the President's room. I want to destroy something that belongs to the man who put me behind bars, that made me miss out on so much of Lily's life.

"That's for missing her prom."

I swing the bat heavily, getting grim satisfaction as it carves a hole in the plaster of the wall.

"And that's for missing her high school graduation."

The bat makes another hole, and this feels fucking good.

Manny put me behind bars. He snitched on me. I was supposed to meet him and his crew for an arms deal. Instead, the cops turned up and caught me with a trunk full of illegal firearms.

I only got a lesser sentence because my sister is the best lawyer in the state.

There's a corridor upstairs with doors leading off to rooms. I try each one, looking for something that Manny would value.

There's a small cupboard at the end, and it's the only door that's locked, which means there must be something worth protecting in there.

I swing my bat hard. It wedges in the door, sending a jolt up my shoulder.

"Motherfucker."

I pull the bat out and swing again. This time, it goes all the way through, making a hole in the door. I reach my hand through, searching for the lock on the other side. My hand finds the doorknob and I turn it, hearing the lock pop open.

There's a rushing sound from the other side of the door, and something comes down on my hand, sending pain shooting up my arm.

"Fuck!" I pull my hand out, and there's blood on my knuckles. Pain sears up my arm, and I see red. Whoever's behind that door is going to pay for this.

My fingers are bent in pain, and I can't grip the baseball bat properly, but I raise it as best I can and open the door.

Someone rushes me. A small ball of fury, hissing at me, all hair and nails, scratching at my arms as they knock me off balance.

I step back, pinned against the other side of the corridor. My bat drops to the floor as I wrestle with the wild cat that's tearing at my skin with her nails.

I know it's a woman because she smells good. Her long hair is wild, and every time it whips around my face, I get a whiff of the floral scent of whatever shampoo she uses.

She's got her legs wrapped around me while her fingers claw at my neck. My head tilts back so she can't scratch my face, and I use my arms to try to wrestle her off. But with my injured hand, it's hard to get a grip on her.

She's fighting with everything she's got, like a cornered animal.

"I'm not gonna hurt you."

I try to calm her down, but it only makes her more irate. I don't want to hurt her, but I need to get her off me before she finds an eyeball with one of those nails.

"I need you to calm down."

I try to warn her, but she still gives a surprised oomph when I drop to my knees and roll her onto the floor.

Now I'm pinning her down, holding her still with my one good arm. Her hair falls off her face, and for the first time, I get a proper look at my attacker.

She's got full, youthful lips, deep red where she's been biting them. Her skin is smooth and tanned, and her wide, dark eyes cast around the room wildly.

My breath catches in my throat. My blood roars in my ears.

*Mine.*

The word echoes in my head, pounds in my heart, and reverberates through my very soul.

*Mine, Mine, Mine.*

It's a clear chant in my head that I'm sure she must hear. And maybe she does because her eyes find mine. She stills for a moment, and we stare at each other.

Her look is pure terror, and a flash of anger goes through me, wondering what she's so frightened off.

"I'm not going to hurt you."

I keep my voice steady and calm, like how you'd talk to a frightened animal, and it seems to work.

Her eyes stay on me, and her breathing slows. I can

feel the swell of her breasts under me with each ragged breath. And help me, God, but I can't help but glance down to peek at the soft mounds that are billowing up and down as she breathes.

Her top has come unbuttoned, and the white lace of her bra is on show, framing two soft pillowy breasts.

My body responds instantly. And she must feel it because the fight comes back into her. She kicks her knee up, and I duck out the way before she can get me in the goods.

The woman rolls out from under me, and I grab her by the ankle before she can escape. She gives a whimper as I drag her back and pin her under me again.

This time, I pin her legs down with my thighs as I hold her hands over her head.

She looks beautiful splayed out on the ground. More than beautiful. The blood rushes south, and I have to look away. I have to block the sight of her below me, the scent of her filling my nostrils. Because I'm not an animal and because I recognize this girl. Although she's not a girl anymore, now clearly a woman. She's Scarlett, Manny's daughter.

"I'm not going to hurt you, Scarlett."

Her eyes widen when I say her name, and her nostrils flare. "My father will find you."

She spits the words with such venom that spittle lands on my lips. I flick my tongue out, tasting her on me. Salty and sweet.

"I'm counting on it."

She breathes hard, but when I help her to her feet, she doesn't resist.

Keeping one hand grasped around Scarlett's wrists, I look into what I thought was a closet, the room where Scarlett was hiding. There's a mattress on the floor and a shelf with a few books and a small stack of folded clothes.

"This your room?"

She sticks her chin out defiantly, not giving me an answer. But the way her cheeks flush red tells me everything I need to know.

Manny lets his daughter sleep in a closet. The guy doesn't deserve her.

The sounds of crashing from downstairs have faded, and Jesse appears at the top of the stairs. "Time to go, Pres."

"I guess I'll be the one who has to clean this mess up," Scarlett huffs.

"Not this time, darling."

I lift her off her feet, and she gives a squeal. She's curvy but she's short, and I toss her over my shoulder like a sack of potatoes.

"What are you doing?" Scarlett gives an indignant huff.

I don't answer her because it's obvious what I'm doing. I'm taking her.

"Put me down." Scarlett wriggles on my shoulder,

and her small fists pummel my back. I stride down the stairs to where the guys are waiting.

"Who's the girl?" Lyle asks.

I wrap my arms around Scarlett's jean-clad thighs, pinning her in place.

"She's my revenge."

To keep reading visit:
mybook.to/UCBikersRevenge

# GET YOUR FREE BOOK

Sign up to the Sadie King mailing list for a FREE book!

You'll be the first to hear about exclusive offers, bonus content and all the news from Sadie King.

To claim your free book visit:
www.authorsadieking.com/free

# BOOKS BY SADIE KING

## Maple Springs

Small Town Sisters

Candy's Café

All the Single Dads

Men of Maple Mountain

## Wild Heart Mountain

Wild Heart Mountain: Military Heroes

Wild Heart Mountain: Wild Riders MC

## Sunset Coast

Underground Crows MC

Sunset Security

Men of the Sea

The Thief's Lover

The Henchman's Obsession

The Hitman's Redemption

For a full list of titles check out the Sadie King website

www.authorsadieking.com

# ABOUT THE AUTHOR

Sadie King is a USA Today Best Selling Author of short instalove romance.

She lives in New Zealand with her ex-military husband and raucous young son.

When she's not writing she loves catching waves with her son, running along the beach, and good wine, preferably drunk with a book in hand.

Keep in touch when you sign up for her newsletter. You'll even snag yourself a free short romance!

www.authorsadieking.com/free

www.ingramcontent.com/pod-product-compliance
Lightning Source LLC
Chambersburg PA
CBHW051826130726
47987CB00003B/1425